# TBH, This Is
# SO Awkward

# TBH, This Is SO Awkward

SCHOLASTIC INC.

LISA GREENWALD

ISBN 978-1-338-55608-7

12 11 10 9 8 7 6 5 4 3 2          19 20 21 22 23 24

Printed in the U.S.A.                    23

First Scholastic printing, February 2019

Typography by Aurora Parlagreco

For Hazel

# BFFAE

**CECILY**

I know we will c each other @ bus in 3 min but doesn't it feel like we've been out of school for soooooo long ⁉️

Scared 2 go back 😲 😲

**GABRIELLE**

🐧 Yes! Running late

Hold bus 4 me!!! 🚀

**PRIANKA**

Already here! Hurry!! 🤍

1

## Sixth-Grade English
## New Year's Resolutions

On the back of this page, please write a letter to yourself with your New Year's resolutions. Be as honest as possible. You are the only one who will see it. We will mail it back to you in December so you can see the progress you made over the course of the year.

Good luck and have fun!

Dear Self:

Ummm. This is so awkward. So... what are my New Year's resolutions? Well, I want to do well in school, maybe all A's, even. I also want to make new friends, but still stay friends with my BFFs, Pri and Cece. Maybe I will run for student council or something, too. Wow—this is a lot to do in one year. I'm tired now! OK, bye, Self, LOL!

xoxox Gabs

Gabs. Do you have any clue what Mr. D is talking about? xo Pri     PRI! Literally no clue. :( xoxo Gabs

## DOLPHIN SQUAD

P   C   G

**PRIANKA**

Sneaking to use fone in 2nd fl b-room

Maybe u will sneak 2

How's 1st day back

**CECILY**

U sent that text 4ever ago—just got it

We r allowed 2 use phones in sci this sem 📱

Mr. D made special app 4 labs 📱📱📱📱

3

Dear Cecily,

Happy New Year! Hee hee. I have a New Year's goal and a New Year's resolution. My goal is to get the highest average in the grade, and keep up with Ingrid. It's hard having an older sister who is a genius. My resolution is to not get so stressed when big projects are assigned. Also to volunteer more. And maybe convince Mom and Dad that we should adopt a shelter dog.

Love, ME

## READING LOG

Hi, Reading Log Partner Gabrielle! My email is: victoriasparkles11@gmail.com and my phone number is 203-555-2792. Bye!

—Victoria

ugh, GABS! i am so mad we aren't reading lab partners this semester. i am stuck with talon corbet! :( xo Pri

I know, Pri!! I think Ms. Marburn split us up on purpose! UNFAIR! xoxox Gabs

Dear Victoria Grace Melford,

My New Year's resolution is to survive this. My parents are the absolute meanest in the entire world to make me move in the middle of the school year. Seriously, who does that? My dad should've just stayed in Philadelphia for the rest of the year. But no, we had to move and now I am stuck here knowing nobody. So yeah, I don't care about New Year's resolutions. I just want to survive this torture.

Sincerely,

Victoria Grace Melford

**From:** Gabrielle Katz
**To:** Prianka Basak, Cecily Anderson
**Subject:** COMPUTER LAB! YAYYY!!!

Hi, girlies!!!!

I'm in Ms. Pinelli's computer lab right now and we're learning how to get our notes and homework off the new school system they installed over break. Do you know it's called Sestina? So fancy! But of course I took a break to email you guys! I LOVE YOUUUUU!!!!! Write back ASAP. Or text. OR see you on the bus!

xoxoxoxoxoxo FOREVER,
Gabs


Dear myself:
Hi, Prianka! How are you? I'm good, Prianka.
Nice to hear from you. HAHA! I crack myself
up. OK, time for New Year's resolutions! Umm.

Basically my New Year's resolution is to make my bed every day, keep my room clean so Mom doesn't freak, and pretty much be the most awesome girl in the grade.

Love, Prianka

 **4EVER**

P C G

CECILY

Did we all survive 1st day? Sorry I missed bus ride home but I got the boots! 👢👢👢

GABRIELLE

Barely survived 😫 all this happened

1. Pri & I got caught passing notes in English 🙊

2. Ms. Marburn said to consider it a warning

3. We r reading THE HUNDRED DRESSES

It's Ms. M's fave! YIPPEE 👏 👏 👏 👏

CECILY

Oh so jeal!!! 🙍‍♀️

PRIANKA

Hate how they change scheds each sem

Only 1 study hall now 😡 😡 😡

CECILY

I don't have any classes w/ M girls this sem, do u

PRIANKA

Just saw them @ lunch

All wore same mint green uneven tee

So matchy matchy 😼 😼

**GABRIELLE**

Ewwww

I didn't see that

**CECILY**

Should we match tomorrow

JK 😂 😂

**GABRIELLE**

LOL 😂

**PRIANKA**

I gotta start hw

Mom is already nagging me & have Bal Vihar class laterz 📚 📚

**CECILY**

Mwah 🤍 😘

**GABRIELLE**

TATA xo

Cece!! U HAVE A BOY BADMINTON PARTNER

GABS!! U R DOING HAND NOTES AGAIN!!!
MY MOM WILL BE SO MAD!!!

ONLY WAY TO PASS NOTES
IN GYM–NO PAPER!

**From:** Victoria Melford
**To:** Kimberly Higgins, Nicole Landenor
**Subject:** MISSING YOU!!

Dear Kim and Nicole:

I miss you guys so much. I am so mad that my parents made us move. Isn't it illegal to make your daughter move schools midyear??? So far my new school is terrible. No one talks to me! I mean, I know it was only the first day. But I had nowhere to sit for lunch. I just sat at the end of a table and ate silently. :(

Can we please plan a sleepover over spring break? Tell me everything that's going on. Maybe I can convince my parents to move back.

xoxo Victoria

---

Dear Diary,

I like Colin so much. I know you already know this, because, duh, I've written it a million times. I want to tell my friends I like him but I'm so scared. We don't talk about boys like that ever. I wonder if Colin will ever like me. Or if he'll ever know I like him. :( And guess what? Colin is Cecily's badminton partner!!!

Love,
Gabby

---

**SQUAD**

P   C   G

**PRIANKA**

U guys r never gonna believe this

Remember that kid Vishal who goes 2 Bal Vihar with me

He switched 2 Yorkville from West End

**GABRIELLE**

R u serious

Midyear ⁉️

**PRIANKA**

IDK. My mom said something about a math program here

Pos, he's a math genius

12

**CECILY**

Wait just got back from store

R u serious

Kid who played in Little League World Series & u made me watch but he was a benchwarmer ⚾⚾⚾

**PRIANKA**

Yes that kid Vishal

Funny, right 😂

**CECILY**

Totes

Snacks for sat sleepover: soft batch cookies, swedish fish, baked lays, doritos, hershey's miniatures, iced tea, and Sprite

& I can always get more 🌀

GABRIELLE

YUM

Thank u

PRIANKA

YAY SO EXCITED

CECILY

See u 2 mañana

PRIANKA

Smooches 💋💋💋

GABRIELLE

Nighty night 😴 🌙 zᶻ

14

## READING LOG

Hi, Victoria—Here is my reading log. I only read six pages last night. This is my 1st time reading this book. Have you read it before? How does Wanda stay so calm? If u have questions about my notes, let me know. K bye.
                                        —Gabby

**From:** Cecily Anderson
**To:** Gabrielle Katz, Prianka Basak
**Subject:** Hi from 7th period study hall

Hi, friends!

I'm writing this from study hall. We're allowed to use computers today. Mara had to change her schedule because she got moved into honors math, and now she's in study hall with me. But she's not so bad. Don't roll your eyes, Pri! HAHA. SO excited for our sleepover. 1 more day!

xoxo Cece

**From:** Vishal Gobin
**To:** Prianka Basak
**Subject:** Hi

Dear Prianka,

Sorry I didn't have time to answer your question at Bal Vihar. I am only here for the rest of this year probably. There is a trial program where they want to let kids take classes at both schools for middle and high school and I signed up to test it out. It's weird. The cafeteria hot dog was probably a bad choice.

Hope you are having a nice day.

Sincerely,
Vishal

## Prianka, Cecily

PRIANKA

U think Gabs is acting weird?

CECILY

4 a sec I thought she was on this group text

Heart pounding

PRIANKA

Would not be that stupid, thankyouverymuch 🙄

So do u ⁉️ 😦

CECILY

Ummm

We need to stash phones the sec we hear her flush, k

We r texting behind her back @ a sleepover

This is bad

PRIANKA

K

Answer me

CECILY

IDK

I feel bad talking bout her, even over text

PRIANKA

K

Sorry

Just worried

CECILY

K she flushed

Put phone away

Dear Diary,

I couldn't write in you last night because I slept
over at Cecily's house. It was fun but I felt like I
had too many secrets. One, the Colin thing. Two,
that we may be moving before the summer. They are
my BFFs, but I couldn't bring it up. You are the
only one who knows this stuff. I'm tired now. Bye.

Love,

Gabby

# THE  MUSKETEERS

P  C  G

**CECILY**

Guys we need 2 decide what club 2 join this sem

**GABRIELLE**

Complicated bc I'm doing 1 night @ my dad's & 1 night @ my mom's now

Pickup times & buses & stuff . . . UGH

Maybe chorus?

Think they'll pick T-Swift songs?

**CECILY**

Prob

Mrs. Sempra likes to do current stuff

Ingrid always sang pop songs & stuff

Do it

GABRIELLE

K yeah

Fun 👏

PRIANKA

Now I wanna do chorus

Can we do more than 1 🙇

CECILY

Maybe, let's ask

We can all do chorus 2gether

That could be great 🎤 👯

GABRIELLE

We need a cool name tho

Like "Shake It Off Sisters" or something . . .

Ya know

Is there an emoji for 3 girls ⁉️

👧👧 👧👧 👧👧

PRIANKA

Yeah let's brainstorm

I gtg

Madre calling me 2 set table

Later, luvies! 💘

CECILY

Ciao 〰️

GABRIELLE

Bye bye mwah

# Cecily, Victoria

C    V

**VICTORIA**

**CECILY**

Who is this

**VICTORIA**

Victoria

From homeroom

I was going over class list Ms. Enarack handed out & I saw ur # & figured I'd text

**CECILY**

Oh hi

Do u like dogs or something

**VICTORIA**

yup luv them 🖤 🖤 🖤

CECILY

Cool

VICTORIA

K um bye

FUN TO TEXT W/ U!!!!!!!!!!

CECILY

K bye

**THE GIRLS** ♥ ♥ ♥ ♥ ♥ ♥

CECILY

Guys, guess what happened when I was waiting for my mom 2 pick me up after Spanish extra help

GABRIELLE

???

**PRIANKA**

Tell us

Y r u taking so long !!!!

**CECILY**

So u know how Ingrid said middle school valentine's dance is like major deal . . . 🤍

**GABRIELLE**

Yea GET TO THE POINT

**CECILY**

So Mrs. Lakely was leaving school & going 2 her car & she told me she's fac advisor 4 the dance again

& she remembered how Ingrid was such a huge help for it 2 years ago . . .

And she wants me 2 help organize a committee

**PRIANKA**

R U SERIOUS RIGHT NOW ⁉️

**CECILY**

YES YES YES YES

Pays to have a fab older sis

**GABRIELLE**

OMG! This means we can literally RUN the biggest event of our lives so far

Like we are in charge

**CECILY**

Haha yeah guess so

I mean we'll need 2 ask other people 2 join & stuff

Make posters & have a meeting

It can't just be us 3 👩👩👩

GABRIELLE

Right 👍

PRIANKA

Soo cool

K gtg get ready 4 bed

C u at bus 1st thing in morn

Smooches 💋 💋

CECILY

MWAH 😍 😍 XOXO

GABRIELLE

XOXOXO 2 infinity 💖 🤍 🖤 💖 🤍 🖤

WE CRUSHED THAT BADMINTON GAME!!!!!!!!!! —Colin

I KNOW!!! GO TEAM Cs!!!! —Cecily

## LUCKY

P   C   G

**PRIANKA**

We r luckiest peeps in the world

Did u see how long wait list was 4 chorus

How did we get so lucky

**GABRIELLE**

IHNC honestly 🙌🏻 🙌🏻 👏🏻

**CECILY**

I know & Mrs. Sempra loved idea 4 our trio
4 solos & stuff

She was totes into it 👊 👊 👊 👊 👊

GABRIELLE

Rlly ❓

U saw her ‼️⁉️‼️

CECILY

She was subbing 4 homeroom today

I feel bad because new girl Victoria didn't get picked

She was sobbing 🙀😔😥🙀😔😥 in homeroom

GABRIELLE

Oh

She is my reading log buddy 📖 📖

PRIANKA

Sad for Victoria 😥

CECILY

She says she really misses her friends at her old school 😕 😫

PRIANKA

Oh sad 😔 😔

GABRIELLE

BTW when is 1st dance comm meeting 💃 💃 💃

CECILY

I need to finalize w/ Mrs. Lakely

Prob next week

Guys, Victoria asked for ur cell #s . . . 📱

GABRIELLE

Umm . . .

She already has mine from homeroom

PRIANKA

Yeah & I don't even know her

CECILY

She's in our gym class right

GABRIELLE

Guys, can we get back 2 the dance comm disc?

CECILY

K let's make list of songs we may wanna do 4 chorus & then we can bring to Mrs. Sempra

& we can start practicing

GABRIELLE

K

Gonna go work on list & text 2 u guys

**From:** Kimberly Higgins
**To:** Victoria Melford
**Subject:** I MISS YOU

Victoria,

I miss you so much. School isn't the same without your weird lunches and your crazy hairstyles. Are you still bringing cold eggplant pizza for lunch? What are your new friends like? Are the classes hard? We miss you so much. Write back ASAP.

Lots of love,
Kim

# LUVIES

**PRIANKA**

Wait 1 q

This is 4 spring concert . . .

So we need cheery, summery songs?

**CECILY**

Yup I think so

**PRIANKA**

K ☑

## Cecily, Victoria

C    V

**VICTORIA**

Does this emoji girl look like me?

**CECILY**

Ummm kinda

But u have brown hair

**VICTORIA**

I KNOW

**CECILY**

I gtg back 2 studying

C ya in homeroom

**VICTORIA**

OK byeeeeeee

## Gabrielle, Victoria

**VICTORIA**

Hi! We can do reading log notes over text? 🖨️

**GABRIELLE**

I think it has to be like written on paper

Isn't that what Ms. Marburn said? 📝📝

**VICTORIA**

IDK

Dear Diary,

I forgot to tell you there is a middle school dance! And I am going to be on the planning committee! I am so excited. I wonder if Colin will ask me to dance. Or maybe I can ask him. I don't know how any of that works. I wish I had an older sister to ask. :(

Love,
Gabby

🎤🎤🎤 **GIRLZZZ**

P   C   G

GABRIELLE

 ICB, M girls wanna b chorus trio 2!

PRIANKA

I can

M girls always think they r stars of everything ⭐ ✨ ⭐ ⭐ ✴️ ⭐

CECILY

Can I say that I don't think they r as bad as they used to b

They r in all my classes & they r actually kinda nice now.

PRIANKA

NO 🙈 🙈

GABRIELLE

NO U CANNOT 🆖 🆖

CECILY

Sheesh k

GABRIELLE

When did M girls become a thing n e way

I mean y r they even friends & popular & stuff 🙉🙉 🙉🙉

PRIANKA

Bc all their names start with M & they think they r cool 🙀

CECILY

Maybe

PRIANKA

I can't figure it out 🙄

CECILY

Let's not waste time worrying about them & just be the awesomest peeps we can b 🐤 🐤 🐤

PRIANKA

Cece is a motivational speaker now! 📡 📢

GABRIELLE

Hahahahahaah totes

PEEPSQUAD 🐤 🐤 🐤

CECILY

LOL LOL PEEPSQUAD gtg do hw 🐤 🐤 🐣 📚 📚

**PRIANKA**

LOL laterz

**GABRIELLE**

Bye

COME AND JOIN THE PLANNING
COMMITTEE FOR THE MIDDLE SCHOOL
VALENTINE'S DAY DANCE!

Where: The Cafeteria
When: Thursday 1/15 After School
Who: HOPEFULLY YOU!

Questions: Email Cecily Anderson
candycorn413@gmail.com

## READING LOG

Gabby—I feel the worst for Maddie, because she has to go along with Peggy . . . she wouldn't be this way on her own, ya know? Are you doing the Valentine's dance planning thing? I know this is just supposed to be for reading log notes, but I was curious. Let me know. —Victoria ♡♡♡

V—I know! I love Maddie! I think I am gonna go to the meeting. I'm not sure, though. OK, I am going to look over your reading log notes. You read fast! –Gabby

# THE BEST SQUAD IN THE WORLD

P  C  G

**PRIANKA**

Did any1 eat that green bean salad @ lunch 2day?

**CECILY**

No . . . Y?

**PRIANKA**

Just checking

Stomach feels a bit off.

**GABRIELLE**

Never eat anything green in school caf

**PRIANKA**

Why'd I never know that rule

**GABRIELLE**

IHNC

Good luck

**CECILY**

Xoxo

# BFFAEAEAEAEAEAEAEAEAE

P  C  G

**PRIANKA**

What did I miss in school 2day

Doc doesn't think food poisoning from green bean salad fyi

😟 😔 😣 😤 😝

**CECILY**

Phew

Umm u didn't miss much

No after-school chorus bc Mrs. Sempra out sick

Pos she ate green bean salad 2?

Need to investigate 👓 😳 👓 😳 👓

Peeps r signing up for dance comm 🐰 🐰 🐰 🐰

GABRIELLE

Who??

CECILY

Um well Keri Harvey & her BFFs + lot of girls IDK

Oh that kid Vishal sent me an email that he's comin

& Colin Hayes & Jared Remington r coming 2 👏 👏 👏

PRIANKA

rlly?

**PRIANKA**

Gonna be big committee 👏 👏 🎉

**CECILY**

Yeah . . . Fun, right? ✌️

**PRIANKA**

Def! 👍

**CECILY**

I gtg help my mom fold laundry 👕 👕

Feel better, Pri 💐 😘


**From:** Victoria Melford
**To:** Kimberly Higgins, Nicole Landenor
**Subject:** Dance??

Do you guys have a Valentine's Day dance?
We have one here, and I am signing up to be
on the committee.

xo Victoria

P   C   G

**GABRIELLE**

This is what my mom made for din

Barf

**CECILY**

What is that

(We had spaghetti)

**GABRIELLE**

Meat & tomato sauce? All mushy . . .

Like a taco w/o shell

45

Or a meatball but not a ball IDK

Crying 😭 😭

PRIANKA

My stomach is still too iffy to see photo like that . . .

Dear Diary,

Cecily just told us that Colin signed up for the dance committee. I AM FREAKING OUT. I am going to be so close to him, working on this, what if I forget how to talk? I NEED HELP. Should I tell my friends I like him?

Love,
Gabby

# DANCE GIRLS 4EVA

( P )  ( C )  ( G )

CECILY

I know u guys will see email but 1st dance planning meeting is Thurs after school 🐧 🐧🐧🐧🐧

GABRIELLE

CECILY

So excited!!!!!

Also M girls did not sign up

Said they r "too busy" 😱 😱

PRIANKA

Whatev

M girls prob think they r 2 cool for dance

So this is big

Need to plan my outfit & actually brush my hair that morn . . . 💇

CECILY

Gonna be great but u guys need 2 bring ideas 2 meeting, k?

Like what we should do for theme & snacks & stuff 🎉 🎉 🎉 🍪 🍩 🍨

GABRIELLE

On it ☑️

CECILY

1 more thing

Victoria joined . . .

GABRIELLE

B

BLARGHEJKWJRKEJHWERHIUEWH1R!!

CECILY

Don't be mean

PRIANKA

She's really weird, Cece

CECILY

K but whatev

We can be nice to her

Bye bye, girls

Hw time

GABRIELLE

ILYSM

49

# Unknown, Gabrielle

What pgs do we need 2 do for math ÷ — ➕ ✖ -Colin

GABRIELLE

How did u get my #

18-23, odd

COLIN

On class list Mr. Boskello passed around

My friends never write down the hw

Lost my planner thx

## Cecily, Victoria

**VICTORIA**

Can't wait 2 talk bout dance!! 💃🕺💃

**CECILY**

Ya

**VICTORIA**

Do u want to start a group text so we can all discuss where we r going 4 dresses? 👗
👗👗👗

**CECILY**

Let's just talk at meeting, k?

**VICTORIA**

BUT WE NEED 2 SHOP 2GETHER!!!
👗👚👗👚

**CECILY**

I am really behind in math hw

Sorry, Victoria

C u tm

VICTORIA

U are always doing hw

K

# Prianka, Cecily

P · C

PRIANKA

Cece, u there?

CECILY

Ya what's up?

Finishing sci lab

PRIANKA

I think Gabs really may be moving soon

It's happening

Huh?

Y?

PRIANKA

We ran into her mom @ grocery store . . .

But I think there's a chance we can convince her Gabs needs 2 stay & finish the yr

CECILY

Ok . . . My throat hurts all of a sudden

What will we do w/o Gabs? & y hasn't she talked to us about it? 😤 😩 😢 😿 😩 😢

PRIANKA

I dunno

We need her 2 stay 🙏 🙇

Let's talk tomrw after assembly

K nighty night

Victoria wants us all 2 go shopping 2gether
4 the dance & text about it

NOOOOOO

Dear Diary,

Colin texted me about the math homework. I don't know what this means. I am going to save the text forever. He never, ever talks to me in person. But maybe he will now. Maybe we can just talk about math.

Love,
Gabby

## Unknown, Prianka

NO CALLER ID

Buttcheeks

PRIANKA

??? Who is this???

NO CALLER ID
U have to guess

PRIANKA
Ummm Ingrid

NO CALLER ID
Who?

No, not Ingrid

PRIANKA
Kamal?

NO CALLER ID
No

PRIANKA
Ummm IHNC

NO CALLER ID
It's Vishal

PRIANKA
Oh um hi

Putting ur # in my fone so u can never do that again

Fine but I can always get new #

Not that easy

We'll see bout that . . .

Dear Gabby, I know we're only reading log partners but I don't understand why you and your friends never write back to my group texts. Did I do something wrong? Please explain. xoxo Victoria  ☆ ☆ ☆

Hi, Victoria,
You didn't do anything wrong. Sometimes we forget to write back. —Gabby

## Mom, Gabrielle

GABRIELLE

Mom, I am so mad at u

I refuse to talk to u in person

No way I am moving with u 2 Aspen

Yorkville is my home.

Will live here by myself if I have 2

I'll move in w/ Cecily or Prianka

**MOM**

Dear Gabrielle, I am willing to discuss this with you calmly, when you are ready. I love you. Mom

## DANCE DANCE DANCE

P C G V

**VICTORIA**

Hiiiii, guys

Soooooooo excited 4 the dance

**From:** Vishal Gobin
**To:** Prianka Basak
**Subject:** COMPUTER LAB IS SO BORING

WHY IS THIS period so boring? All we do is practice typiNG. DID YOU SIGN UP FOR THE BAL VIHAR carnival? I am trying every font. Bye.


**From:** Prianka Basak
**To:** Vishal Gobin
**Subject:** DON'T GET ME IN TROUBLE

It's not boring. Don't get me in trouble. I love this font, though. Bye.

# MEMO

**From**: Mr. Carransey, Principal, Yorkville Middle School
**To**: ALL SIXTH-GRADE PARENTS
**Re**: Cell phone use in school

I hope the New Year is off to a good start for everyone.

I wanted to remind all of you that phones are not to be used during the school day unless directed by a teacher for an actual assignment.

Also, I encourage you all to speak to your children about social media, who they're texting, and what is taking place in these text conversations. We must open the lines of communication between parents and students when it comes to our ever-changing world of technology. I appreciate your attention to this matter.

Sincerely,
Edward Carransey
Principal
Yorkville Middle School

*Be the change you want to see in the world.—Gandhi*

# BFFFFFFFFF

P C G

GABRIELLE

Where r u guys?

I'm 1st 1 here

CECILY

Coming

Had to pee

PRIANKA

EWWW

I'm so nervous

Hiding in band room 2 get ready 🎶 🎶 🎼

# Cecily, Victoria

**VICTORIA**

R u there?

**CECILY**

**VICTORIA**

Heard u & ur friends talking at the end of the meeting about stuff 4 the dance & I felt really left out 💔 💔

**CECILY**

Oh so sorry - don't feel left out

We r all on the committee & we can all discuss 👭👭👭

**VICTORIA**

I know, but u guys r all so close & I want 2 set up a time 4 us all 2 hang

U never wb 2 my group texts

Isn't this baby angel so cute?

CECILY
Yeah cute

What about this cat 😻

VICTORIA
EVEN CUTER. ✔✔

**From:** Victoria Melford
**To:** Kimberly Higgins, Nicole Landenor
**Subject:** THIS SCHOOL IS CRAZY

Hi, guys—

I hate this school. I went to the dance committee meeting and no one talked to me! I text people and they don't write back! What is going on? I was cool at Bayberry, wasn't I? I mean, not cool cool but, like, normal cool? I feel like everything is backwards here.

I'm in study hall now. So boring. How can I convince my mom to move back?

SMOOCHES! Victoria

## THE GIRLZZZZZ

GABRIELLE

So that was chaotic

CECILY

IK

We'll never agree 2 a theme

& it's like 5 weeks away!!

Also, Victoria really wants 2 hang out w/ us. She keeps asking

I think we should just do it 2 be nice

**PRIANKA**

K I don't think we r being mean to Victoria

But we don't have to hang out w/ her

Also we'll agree on theme

We may just have 2 have anonymous voting or something

Did u c how mad Marissa got when I suggested NYC as the theme

She was like furious

**CECILY**

I guess bc she used to live there when she was like 5, and feels angry she had 2 move 😡😡😡

**PRIANKA**

Maybe but come on - that mad? Ew 😠

**GABRIELLE**

All the boys cared about was food.

Did u notice that?

PRIANKA

Boys always care about food

GABRIELLE

Yeah true

PRIANKA

I gtg we have 1st chorus rehearsal tomrw

Don't forget 💚 🎶 💚

GABRIELLE

ILYSM, girlies.

CECILY

Smooch 😙 😽 😽

PRIANKA

Xoxooxxo

## Cecily, Mara

**MARA**

Cecily, is this your #?

**CECILY**

Yes hi

**MARA**

Hi! Hope it's not weird that I'm texting u

But since u gave out ur number 2 the dance committee . . .

At 1st I didn't want to join but now I do really want to help w/ dance. 👧👧👧

**CECILY**

It's not weird

Also u could just ring my bell

Did u forget u live next door? LOL

68

**MARA**

HAHA. 😼 😼 😼 DUH! OK!

Well see u tomrw!

# THE GIRLZZZZZ

CECILY

Guys, Mara just texted me out of the blue, saying she really does want 2 help with the dance.

PRIANKA

STOP

WHAT???!!! 👀 🔋

GABRIELLE

Y?!?!?

**CECILY**

No idea.

**GABRIELLE**

Cece is gonna become M girl 👧👧👧👧

**CECILY**

Um no

I will not 🤚🤚

**PRIANKA**

K . . .

**VICTORIA**

Hi, Prianka, Gabrielle & Cecily

HIIII!

So excited we can all group text 👯👯👯👯
👯

**PRIANKA**

HELLO? ANY1 THERE?

R we all ignoring Victoria?

WHAT IS GOING ON?

Also, u r never gonna believe this

**CECILY**

What ⁉️❓⁉️❓

**GABRIELLE**

Sorry, I am behind. What's going on?

**PRIANKA**

Vishal is having a boy-girl bday party!

OUR 1st EVER!!!! 👫👫👫

**CECILY**

OMG

**GABRIELLE**

When ❓❓❓

Where ❓❓❓

Are we invited???

TELL ALL NOW ❗❗❗❗

**PRIANKA**

K IDK if we r all invited

I know I am invited . . . Invites are

He's like having a real deal 12th birthday

Who does that

**CECILY**

I guess Vishal 😂 😂

**PRIANKA**

Haha

Right

Pos bc he changed schools & needs to b social

**CECILY**

It's gonna be awesome

But better if we r there obv 👍 👍 👍

**GABRIELLE**

Think M girls will be invited?

**PRIANKA**

I think they will . . .

Did u know Marissa has been talking to Vishal after study hall?

I try to ignore it but it's happening

I mean their dads know each other from college or something, so it's not THAT crazy

But it's still crazy

CECILY

Wait - how do u know about the party

Did u already get the invite

Eavesdropping again? Hee hee

PRIANKA

I had to hear from MY MOM

SO LAME.

GABRIELLE

No offense but that is lame-o 2 the extreme

74

**CECILY**

Gabs come on

Not the nicest response

**GABRIELLE**

Fine sorry

But we need 2 step up our game

If parties r happening we need 2 b the ones 2 find out about them

Ya know

**PRIANKA**

K, Gabs . . . U lead the way.

Bc u know about soooo many parties 🙄

**CECILY**

Guys, stop fighting

Remember we promised we wouldn't fight over text

PRIANKA
Ummm 🤔

CECILY
Yes, u do remember

GABRIELLE
Fine

Sorry, I'm just in bad mood 😣

PRIANKA
Y

GABRIELLE
My mom is still talking about moving 🚚🏠

PRIANKA
K we will make sure you don't move but 1st thing is getting invited 2 the party

So let's meet @ lockers first thing tomw morn & figure out what we r going 2 do 2 get invites

CECILY

K MWAH

GABRIELLE

Xoxo

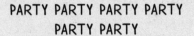

PARTY PARTY PARTY PARTY
PARTY PARTY

Where: Casa de Gobin
(Vishal's pad)
16 Piedmont Drive

When: February 2, 6pm

Why: Last-minute party because
VISHAL IS TURNING 12, YO!

RSVP: VGobs1342@gmail.com

## Prianka, Cecily

CECILY

Pri we need 2 come up with game plan 2 make sure Gabs doesn't move

Like we do 1 thing each day 2 convince her mom 2 stay

PRIANKA

Ummm I like it

But what can we do 🤔

CECILY

Leave note in her mailbox every day with diff reason of y Yorkville is best place 2 live
😀😀😀😀📫📬📫📬

PRIANKA

K!

Or email if we can't make it over there . . .

CECILY

Good backup plan 👏👏 ✓ ✓

**PRIANKA**

Fab

**VICTORIA**

IS ANY1 OUT THERE???? HELLOOOOOO I'VE TEXTED U GUYS SO MANY TIMES & NO 1 RESPONDS!!!!!!!!

DID EVERY1 GET INVITED 2 VISHAL'S PARTY!? Sorry 4 all caps

**From:** Victoria Melford
**To:** Vishal Gobin
**Subject:** PARTY!!!!!!!!!!!!!!!!!!!!!!!!!!!!!!!

Hi, Vishal,

I heard you are having a party. We just moved here and my address isn't in the school directory.

I would love to come to your party.

See you in Global Studies!

Victoria

## SICK CECE

**CECILY**

I don't think u guys r going to see this until way l8r

I'm home puking my guts out

Some1 needs 2 respond 2 Victoria's group text

PLZZZZZZ

## SICK CECE

**CECILY**

Still here

On a puke break

BUT GUESS WHO GOT INVITED TO VISHAL'S PARTY

Obvs u will b 2 . . .

## THE CREW

PRIANKA

Ok, so we r all invited

YAY

Cece, how r u feeling 😦

CECILY

BLARGHSJWKJNDKJSH 🤢🥴

GABRIELLE

Wow, that bad huh? 🙀😪😢

83

CECILY

I may not be back tomw 🐱 . . . & we have dance comm

U guys gotta take over for me, k?

GABRIELLE

Um

I'll try . . .

PRIANKA

We can do this

& YAY TO THIS PARTY

K - we have 2 plan outfits

CECILY

Gtg . . . Sick Cece over here

PRIANKA

FEEL BETTER

GABRIELLE

Feel better, Cece.

# THE CREW 👊 👊 👊

P   C   G

**CECILY**

Um so don't freak out but Mara texted me to see how I'm feeling . . .

Guys, I feel like M girls want 2 be friends w/ us

They r honestly nice I promise 🐰 🐰 🐰 🐰 🐰 🐰

**GABRIELLE**

WHOA

K but u DEK what happened @ lunch 2day!!

**CECILY**

???

**PRIANKA**

⁉️⁉️

85

GABRIELLE

K so there was def a fight b/t M girls

Mara got mad at Marissa saying she was talking 2 Mae behind her back

PRIANKA

HA - this sounds crazy

GABRIELLE

It was

Mrs. Manuso had 2 get involved

& u know that's bad . . .

CECILY

So what happened

?????

GABRIELLE

All 3 of them were crying . . . 😿 😿 😿

Then Mara stopped me on the way 2 math 2 ask me where u were, Cece

CECILY

What? Really?

GABRIELLE

Yup

I think she's trying 2 break away from them

CECILY

No way

M girls are tight as can be

GABRIELLE

I know

Soooooo weird right

CECILY

Well, Mara is the nicest . . .

**PRIANKA**

Just stay away from Marissa

She's the 1 who is in  w/ Vishal

**GABRIELLE**

K whatev

My mom calling me

GTG

**PRIANKA**

BYE 👋

**CECILY**

Hope 2 be back in school tomw

ILY

**From:** Priscilla Melford
**To:** Edward Carransey
**Subject:** Victoria Melford experiencing social cruelty

Dear Mr. Carransey:

My daughter, Victoria (sixth grade), is being excluded at every turn. She is new to the school. As you know, we had to move midyear. Victoria joined the dance committee to meet new friends, but they do not include her in plans outside of school, despite many attempts. She is consistently left out of group texting communication. It is affecting her schoolwork and she is experiencing immense anxiety.

Also, it seems the students are overly concerned about dates for the Valentine's Day dance. This is not appropriate. I do not feel that dates should be allowed for a sixth-grade dance.

I would like to set a meeting with you to

discuss what can be done about these two issues.

Sincerely,
Priscilla Melford

*Live, laugh, love.*

Reason #1 why
you need to stay in
Yorkville:
The best friends in
the world.
♡ xoxo

## Unknown, Prianka

**NO CALLER ID**

Hello Prianka

BARF BRAIN!!!!!!!!

**PRIANKA**

??? Who r u?

## 🧜🧜🧜 CREW

**PRIANKA**

Any1 else get BARF BRAIN text?

**CECILY**

No . . . But stomach bug going around obv

I didn't

PRIANKA

GUYS, this is serious

Mystery texter

PLEASE HELP

Remember what Mr. Carransey said about social cruelty

CECILY

Ask who it is!

PRIANKA

I DID

# BFFFFFFFF

P   C   G

GABRIELLE

Nice note in my mailbox, Pri 📫 📪

PRIANKA

HUH ⁉️

GABRIELLE

I know ur handwriting, silly!

My mom thought it was sweet

PRIANKA

So did it work 😹 😂

GABRIELLE

IDK but thanx 🎇 👹 🎇 👹 🎇

## Unknown, Prianka

NO CALLER ID
**BARF BRAIN**

PRIANKA
**WHO IS THIS??!!**

**ANSWER ME**

**I AM GOING 2 CALL THE POLICE** 🚓🚓🚨👮

NO CALLER ID
Calm down

PRIANKA
**TELL ME**

NO CALLER ID
Ok, it's Vishal

## Vishal, Prianka

VISHAL

Sorry

PRIANKA

Huh . . . Y did u just text me BARF BRAIN

VISHAL

My brother did  from his phone

HAHAHAAHAHAAHAHA

SoRrY

I was using his phone & then he stole it

TOLD U I COULD FIND OTHER NUMBERS

HAHAHAHA

PRIANKA

Bye

**PRIANKA**

It was Vishal's brother . . . WEIRD

**CECILY**

That is weird 😨

**GABRIELLE**

GUYS, u r never going 2 believe this

Ya know how Mrs. Hughes lives next door & my mom and her exercise 2gether sometimes

**CECILY**

Yeah?

**GABRIELLE**

Wellllllllll, some of the moms called school & complained that our grade is getting too crazy with dates & stuff 4 the dance & they may not even allow dates AT ALL 🐶🐶🐶

**PRIANKA**

What!!!!!! That is crazy!!!!!!!!

Cece, did Ingrid's grade have dates?

**CECILY**

Umm . . . I think so.

**GABRIELLE**

Who do u think complained?

**CECILY**

No idea!!!

**PRIANKA**

This is crazy 🙃 🙃

Did u guys tell ur moms we were going to ask boys to the dance

I didn't

MINE would FLIP!

CECILY

I didn't . . . IDC if I bring a date

Do u guys?

I just wanna have fun with every1

GABRIELLE

IDK how to ask some1 2 be my date!!!

My mom would prob freak & then try to make us move even more 🚫➖🚫➖

CECILY

We need 2 get 2 the bottom of this

But here's the thing - peeps don't all have 2 do the same thing

If some1 wants 2 bring a date, fine

If not, also fine

Ya know?

Every1 is going CRAZY. ✋☮✋☮✋☮

PRIANKA
I KNOW

WIGO?!?

madness 😕 😕 😕

CECILY
OK

KEEP CALM, PEOPLE, KEEP CALM

Going to bed now XOX

PRIANKA
Night night 💚 🤍

GABRIELLE
MWAH

**From:** Priscilla Melford
**To:** Sixth-Grade Parents Association
**Subject:** Valentine's Day Dance

Dear fellow parents:

It has come to my attention that some of the students are trying to bring dates to the Valentine's Day dance. I do not feel this is appropriate, and I think the administration needs to get involved.

Please add this to the agenda for the PA meeting on Thursday.

Sincerely,
Priscilla Melford

*Live, laugh, love.*

Dear Diary,

Colin talked to me in math today. He asked when the quiz was. He also asked me if I am going to Vishal's party. I am freaking out. I have to tell my friends I like him, but I am so scared because what if he doesn't like me? I don't know what to do.

Love,
Gabby

# Prianka, Cecily

PRIANKA

Cece, u there? 🩶

CECILY

Doing sci lab

Wuz  ?

PRIANKA

Have u left any more notes

CECILY

Yea but we need 2 keep doing it

My mom had dinner w/ Gabby's mom 2night & I think she really wants 2 move

PRIANKA

NOOOO 😭 😭

**CECILY**

We will keep working on it

Gtg do this lab

Don't be mad, but Mara is coming over after school again tomw

She asked me to hang out

K, promise? Don't be mad 🙏

**PRIANKA**

Calm down

Weren't u the 1 who said to stay calm

I'm not mad

**CECILY**

OK

XOXOX 💔 ❤️

**PRIANKA**

Xo ❤️ ❤️ ❤️ ❤️

Reason #2 to stay in
Yorkville:
The best pizza in the
whole world. Jennie's!
Nothing else will
compare.
♡ xoxo

**From:** Colin Hayes
**To:** Cecily Anderson
**Subject:** BEST BADMINTON PARTNERS EVER

Yo. I am in study hall and had an idea. What if we suggested to Mr. Peeds and the gym department that we start a badminton team? We are so good! I think kids would be into it. And maybe that would help fulfill my community service requirement?

Probably not. HAHAHA.
Peace out,
Colin

## Prianka, Gabrielle

PRIANKA

Hi, Gabs 🩶

GABRIELLE

Hiiiiii

PRIANKA

I think we need emergency sleepover this weekend

Cece is hanging out w/ Mara after school again tomw

Don't tell her I told u

Maybe Cece does want to be friends w/ them . . . & she's trying to break away from us 🙄

And Victoria is trying to hijack us

Don't want 2 be mean 2 her but she is sooooo annoying

GABRIELLE

Ok this is a big deal!!!!!!!!!! 😭 😢 😭 😢 😭

PRIANKA

IK

WE NEED TO FIX THIS! 👍 👍

**From:** Darlene Lakely
**To:** Cecily Anderson
**Subject:** Valentine's Day Dance Logistics

Hi, Cecily,

I wondered if you could meet five to ten minutes before lunch on Wednesday so we can discuss some logistics about the dance.

Thank you,
Mrs. Lakely

## Mara, Cecily

M  C

MARA

Was so much fun 2 hang w/ u 😊 😊

CECILY

 had fun 2!! 👏 👏

**MARA**

Good luck w/ Mrs. Lakely meeting

I'm sure it is nothing major

**CECILY**

Fingers crossed

Also Colin Hayes wants 2 start a badminton team

So funny, right?

**MARA**

THAT WOULD BE SO FUNNY

LMK what happens w/ Lakely

# EMERGENCY SLEEPOVER

!!  !!

P   C   G

GABRIELLE

Sleepover sat?

PRIANKA

CECILY

**From:** Cecily Anderson
**To:** Colin Hayes
**Subject:** Badminton Team

I like your idea. Just so busy now with the dance stuff. But maybe we can do it closer to the spring.

# Victoria, Cecily

**VICTORIA**

Still didn't get invite 2 Vishal's party

I emailed him & he didn't wb

What should I do????

...

**CECILY**

Sometimes  is weird

Don't worry

**VICTORIA**

I AM SO STRESSED

Also ur friends don't respond 2 my group texts

What is wrong w/ me?? 👽 👾

CECILY

Phone dying

Let's talk tomrw

CECILY

U guys, this Victoria thing is making me crazy

She's really hurt

We need 2 respond or just be nice or something

IDK!!!!! 🙏 ☮️ ✌️

PRIANKA

But IDK her!!!! 😑 😮 😑

GABRIELLE

 SAME

TBH I feel bad but we don't have any classes 2gether besides gym + Eng

She asked 2 switch & be my badminton partner but Mr. Peeds said no

I am stuck w/ Becky Willard

She's so much better than I am & I think she hates me

Also, I am already so stressed with hw

CECILY

OK

Let's talk about it @ sleepover 💜💜

READING LOG

It's been nice having a break from reading log, hasn't it? Here are my pages. Can we hang out sometime? —Victoria

I kind of missed reading log, to be honest. I'm really stressed because we may be moving. I feel like Wanda! :( :( :( I'll let u know when I am free to hang. —Gabby

## Cecily, Mara

( C ) ( M )

So the Mrs. Lakely meeting wasn't that crazy but she is concerned about dates thing

She wanted to know what I thought about it

MARA

What do u think ⁇

CECILY

IDK

People r getting kinda crazy.

& some peeps might not have a date . . .

MARA

Yeah. Hmmm . . .

Well, we still have time

I gtg finish English essay

C u tomw 💕

CECILY

Bye bye

**From:** Beverly Flam
**To:** Priscilla Melford
**Subject:** Meeting to discuss Victoria

Dear Mrs. Melford:

I wanted to set up a time to meet in person to discuss how Victoria is adjusting to her new school. Please get back to me at your earliest convenience.

Kind regards,
Beverly Flam

*Peace. It does not mean to be in a place where there is no noise, trouble, or hard work. It means to be in the midst of those things and still be calm in your heart.*
*—Unknown*

# Vishal, Prianka

**VISHAL**

What do u think peeps should do at my party

**PRIANKA**

Ummmm

**VISHAL**

Snacks + video games 🎮 🎮

**PRIANKA**

I never knew there was a video game emoji! COOL!

**VISHAL**

So?

**PRIANKA**

Will try and think of ideas 💡 💡

**From:** Kimberly Higgins
**To:** Victoria Melford
**Subject:** GUESS WHAT?

V-girl:

My phone got taken away bc I got a C in math. But I can still email. LOL!

Guess who asked about you today? Mark Carlyle! Remember him? He was like "I haven't seen Victoria around." And I was like "That's because she moved!"

LOL LOL LOL
LOVE YOU TONS!
K-girl

## Mom, Prianka

MOM

Prianka, get downstairs this instant. Texting seems to be the only way to reach you these days, which is very disappointing. Love, Mom

PRIANKA

???

MOM

Get down here now. Your teacher called and I am very disappointed.

**PRIANKA**

OMG OMG OMG OMG OMG OMG

**CECILY**

??????

**GABRIELLE**

Wuzzzzz

**PRIANKA**

Ms. Peabody called my mom bc Victoria said I am being so mean to her

& my mom said if I don't stop I can't go to Vishal's party or 2 the dance

BUT IT ISN'T EVEN TRUE!!!!!!!!!

**CECILY**

WOW

OMG

GABRIELLE

I KNOW

I don't get this

R we all gonna get calls home!?!?!?

PRIANKA

IDK 😩

# MEMO

**From**: Mr. Carransey, Principal, Yorkville Middle
School
**To**: ALL SIXTH-GRADE STUDENTS

Reminder that we have an assembly immediately
following fifth period TODAY. Please meet in the
auditorium. Thank you.

Sincerely,
Edward Carransey
Principal
Yorkville Middle School

*Be the change you want to see in the world. —Gandhi*

## Vishal, Prianka

**VISHAL**

Who is Victoria

I'm confused

She emailed me

**PRIANKA**

She came from Philly

She's in comp lab with me but IDK her that well

**VISHAL**

OK

**From:** Priscilla Melford
**To:** Aarushi Gobin
**Subject:** Our children

Dear Aarushi:

We haven't met as of yet but we have a mutual friend—Joy Greely—and she speaks very highly of you. I wanted to get in touch regarding your son Vishal's party. I want my daughter, Victoria, to handle her personal matters on her own, so I instructed her to email Vishal, but she has not heard back. She will be very disappointed if she is not invited to his party. I wondered if an exception could be made just this once, as she is still adjusting to a new school.

Thank you,
Priscilla

*Live, laugh, love.*

**SQUADDDDD**

P C G

**PRIANKA**

Soooooo . . . Victoria's mom got my mom's # & now my mom said that if I don't let her come 2 Vishal's party with us then I can't go. 😴 😴

**GABRIELLE**

WHAT ⁉️⁉️⁉️⁉️

**PRIANKA**

I KNOW

How did this even happen

**CECILY**

Guys, it'll be ok

We can all meet @ ice cream place before

Isn't that a block away from where Vishal lives

124

PRIANKA

I guess

I mean, my mom did say she doesn't think
we r being mean but that V's mom really
wants her 2 have friends & she's having
hard time @ new school

CECILY

So it'll be fine

HONESTLY

Better to just be nice

GABRIELLE

FINE

# PARTY PEOPLE

P C G V

**VICTORIA**

OMG U GUYS!!!

SO excited 4 Vishal's party & 2 go 2gether!!!!

**CECILY**

Yay!

GABRIELLE

**PRIANKA**

# THE REAL  SQUAD

GABRIELLE

But does she have to hang out w/ us the whole time??

PRIANKA

Wait, did u just respond to our group text w/ Victoria w/ that????

GABRIELLE

No

I'm not that dumb

PRIANKA

PHEW

CECILY

STAY CALM, PEOPLE

**From:** Nicole Landenor
**To:** Victoria Melford
**Subject:** HAVE SO MUCH FUN!!!!!

I'm in English now and supposed to be writing an essay and I miss you soooooo much!

Kim told me you're going to a boy-girl party. OMG, have so much fun! I want all details after. Did I tell you that Robbie Shenz likes me? I think I like him, too. Okay, bye.

Hugs,
Nic

## Unknown, Victoria

NO CALLER ID

Y R U @ this party

VICTORIA

?? Who is this

NO CALLER ID

U R not friends w/ any1 here

## Mara, Cecily

MARA

I am missing Vishal's party bc I finally got stomach flu every1 had

CECILY

Oh no!

Will miss u

MARA

Thanks, have fun

If I'm better tomw let's discuss the dance

I have ideas

K, feel better

## Prianka, Cecily

PRIANKA

Where r M girls?

Weird I am texting u when u r right here, but I didn't want anyone 2 overhear

CECILY
Hee hee

Mara is sick

PRIANKA
K

130

So I guess the other 2 decided to stay home?

Gabs has been sitting next to Colin 4 like hours now . . . 😲 😲 😲 😲 😏

CECILY
I guess so . . .

Where is Victoria?

PRIANKA
IDK

This party is weird

Vishal texts me all the time but ignoring me here & all he's doing is 🎮 🎮 w/ Jared & those boys

CECILY
Weird party

Let's go soon, k? 🙏 👸

PRIANKA

K

ILY

## Unknown, Victoria

NO CALLER ID

U don't look like U R having fun

Y R U here 👽 👻 😈 👿 👹 👺 💀 👾 👽

VICTORIA

I'm leaving this lame party & I'm telling Mr. Carransey about these texts

## VICNICKIM

**VICTORIA**

U guys, this party is terrible

I hate it

I am getting rude anonymous mystery texts

**NICOLE**

Really ⁉️😪🙀😨

**KIMBERLY**

Ewww 👎🏻👎🏻

**VICTORIA**

Wish I was w/ u guys now 🙀🙀

## PARTY PEOPLE

( P ) ( C ) ( G ) ( V )

**VICTORIA**

My mom is coming to pick me up

IDK where u guys r!

## BFFAEAEAEAEAE

( P ) ( C ) ( G )

**CECILY**

K, so that was def craziest party in history

**PRIANKA**

So glad it's over

Vishal ignored me

I AM SO MAD

Colin talked to me about sports and stuff I didn't care about 😒 😒 😒 😒

I just sat there

CECILY

Phone battery died so I never got that text from Victoria & I didn't even see her leave!

PRIANKA

I didn't see her either & when I took my jacket off

I left 📱 in pocket!

GABRIELLE

Weird we haven't heard from her since party 😬 😬 😬 😬

PRIANKA

IDK

CECILY

??

# MEMO

**From:** Mr. Carransey, Principal, Yorkville Middle School
**To:** ALL SIXTH-GRADE PARENTS
**Re:** Ongoing Social Cruelty

Dear parents:

The cruelty via text message and other electronic communication continues in the sixth-grade class. We must work together to eradicate this problem. I am calling an emergency meeting of administrators, teachers, and parents Thursday evening at 7:00 p.m. I expect to see everyone there. If we cannot solve this very serious problem, the annual Valentine's Day dance will be canceled.

Thank you for your attention to this matter.

Edward Carransey
Principal
Yorkville Middle School

*Be the change you want to see in the world.—Gandhi*

dear colin,
I know it's weird to write a note like this,
but I just need to tell you that you're so cute.
you're the cutest boy in the whole grade, and I
don't think you even know it.
—your secret admirer ♡ ♡   ♡

# DA CREW

P    C    G

**PRIANKA**

Did ur parents tell u what happened @ the
meeting?

**GABRIELLE**

!??

**PRIANKA**

There's an app parents can get where they
can SEE our phones

Like from their phones . . .

CECILY

Uhh. Do u guys have lots of secrets? 😂 😂

PRIANKA

No . . .

GABRIELLE

Noo . . .

CECILY

Guys, they'll prob look once & then get bored

Let's just be extra boring the next few days. 😂 😂

PRIANKA

YES. Thank u, genius Cece.

GABRIELLE

But we are 2 cool 2 be boring. 😉

CECILY

1 other thing

We gotta be super nice to Victoria

Dance will be canceled if parents keep
complaining

PRIANKA

But it's not only us!

& we r not even mean

GABRIELLE

I'm nice 2 her

CECILY

K so group text with VM starts tomorrow

Haha her initials r VM like voicemail . . .
😂😂

GABRIELLE

But we can't be like over the top nicey

I mean, ya know . . .

PRIANKA

K, whatev it takes

CECILY

LOL

GABRIELLE

Mwah

Bye

See you tomw 🖤 🖤 🖤

Reasons #3, #4, #5
····▶ to stay in Yorkville: ◀····
(I think, I lost count)
Yorkville Pool, ice
cream at Waverly's,
sunsets over the river.
♡ xoxo

## Colin, Gabrielle

COLIN

Yo I found a super weird secret note in my locker

GABRIELLE

Wha??

COLIN

IDK

Like secret admirer or something

GABRIELLE

Really? Weird!!

COLIN

Do u know anyone who likes me

GABRIELLE

Uhhh . . . IHNC

COLIN

Ok, well, if u find out let me know

GABRIELLE

K

Dear Diary,

I did something crazy and left a note in Colin's locker and now I am totally regretting it. Why did I do it? I don't know. He talked to me at the party and I just had to do something. ACK. This is hell.

Love,
Gabby

**From:** Colin Hayes
**To:** Cecily Anderson
**Subject:** Note

Yo badminton partner—I got a secret admirer note. Do you know who it could be?

**From:** Diana Katz
**To:** Manjula Basak, Elizabeth Anderson
**Subject:** App?

Hi, ladies,

Did you download this app? It seems so confusing. I did something terrible and snooped in G's diary, and it's all about some boy, Colin? What is happening? We need dinner ASAP to figure these girls out. Ahhh—remember when they were babies? The good old days. Now diapers and colic and naps seem easy . . .

xoxo Diana

# BABEZZZ

P   C   G

**PRIANKA**

Ladies . . .

**CECILY**

Hey wut  ?

**PRIANKA**

I'm gonna start group text with VM, k?

**CECILY**

U guys hear about secret note in Colin's locker

**GABRIELLE**

I guess he has a secret admirer

? 🔘 ?

Whatevs 🖤🖤

PRIANKA

Bet it's 1 of M girls

Cece, u gotta find out from Mara

CECILY

U think?

They don't even rlly know Colin

GABRIELLE

He's obvi cutest kid in the grade . . .
😃😃😃😎

PRIANKA

He is??? 😂 😂

GABRIELLE

IDK

CECILY

K

Just start group chat w/ V

**From:** Cecily Anderson
**To:** Colin Hayes
**Subject:** RE: Note

Hi, Badminton Partner—

No idea who sent you the note! Mysterious . . .

**PRIANKA**

Just wanted to say hey 👋

**CECILY**

HEY HEY! 👋

**GABRIELLE**

Hiiiii 👋

**PRIANKA**

Victoria, r u there?

**VICTORIA**

Hi! 🐤🥝🌴🌳🌲🍌🍇🍎🍟🍎🍐

**PRIANKA**

Soo what's going on??? 🐳🐳🐳

**VICTORIA**

Nada 🌑🌒🌓🌔🌕🌖🌗🌘🌙⭐🌟☁️

 **BFFs**

**PRIANKA**

Guys, there is nothing to text w/ her about . . .

**CECILY**

U r going 2 get confused about which text u r on & say something by mistake 💊💊

**PRIANKA**

No

I won't

It's ok

GABRIELLE

I'll ask if she knows about the colin note

**GIRLIESSSSS**

(P) (C) (G) (V)

GABRIELLE

Do u guys have any idea who sent colin that note

PRIANKA

NOPE

CECILY

Me neither

So weird

VICTORIA

I heard about this in math

So weird

He's like super serious about finding out who sent it

GABRIELLE

So crazy

V, who do u think it is

VICTORIA

IDK

Maybe Kelly O'Neal

GABRIELLE

WHAT ⁉️

No way 🚫 ⛔

VICTORIA

IDK

I just said maybe . . .

 **BFFs**

PRIANKA

She has no idea what she is talking about

CECILY

Pri, stop doing side chats

GABRIELLE

Kelly O'Neal does not like Colin

That's like, craziness . . .

I don't think she likes any1

She doesn't even really talk

PRIANKA

I KNOW

CECILY

Guys, u r being really mean

Aren't our moms looking at our phones w/ that app

WIGO

PRIANKA

UGH this feels so stressful 😠 😠 😠 😠

**GIRLIESSSSS** 💅 💅 💅

P  C  G  V

PRIANKA

I don't think Kelly O'Neal knows who Colin is

🙈 🙊 🙉

**VICTORIA**

They sit next to each other in Spanish 👫👬👫

**PRIANKA**

Oh

**CECILY**

So what else is going on 👣👣

**GABRIELLE**

Nada

So much math hw

Cryinngggggggg

📚📚📚📚

**VICTORIA**

I knowwwwwwwwwwwwwwwwwwwwww

**PRIANKA**

Uhhh, Victoria is SO annoying guys

Please

Can this end?

**VICTORIA**

???

 **BFFs**

P   C   G

**CECILY**

PRIANKA ASHWINI BASAK

DO U SEE WHAT U JUST DID???

**PRIANKA**

OMG I thought that was other group text

I feel soooooo bad

GABRIELLE

OMG what r we going to do 🐺 🐺

CECILY

We aren't gonna do anything, gabs

Pri has to figure this out

I gtg

GABRIELLE

Uhhh ok

Oops, good luck, Pri

# GIRLIESSSSS

P  C  G  V

**PRIANKA**

I'm so sorry Victoria

My bro was annoying me & I got confused & meant to send that about my bro . . .

I typed ur name by mistake

**VICTORIA**

Ok yeah right

I gtg

**PRIANKA**

SO SORRY

## Colin, Gabrielle

**COLIN**

Soooo . . . Did u find anything out about who wrote that letter?

**GABRIELLE**

No

IHNC

Y r u asking me

**COLIN**

Bc u know stuff, Gabs . . .

I need ur help 👍 👍

# ILY2SM

P  C  G

GABRIELLE

Guys, I have to tell u something . . .

CECILY

??

GABRIELLE

K, so . . . Ready?

CECILY

Ready go puhlease !!!!

GABRIELLE

K, so I was the 1 who sent anon note to Colin bc I've liked him 4 so long & I'm sorry I never told u guys but I was so embarrassed

He keeps texting me to see if I know who sent it

GABRIELLE

HE·CALLED ME GABS!!!

CECILY

UMMMM

OMG

THIS IS A LOT TO DIGEST

GABRIELLE

Pri?

CECILY

I think her phone got taken away . . .

Overheard her telling Vishal in the hallway

She tried 2 tell me but I'm not talking 2 her right now

GABRIELLE

Ok

Everything feels so sad

CECILY

R u going to tell Colin it was u??

GABRIELLE

IDK

CECILY

I gtg

GABRIELLE

CECILY

See u tomw

# Colin, Gabrielle

COLIN

U there?

GABRIELLE

Yup

COLIN

See if u can find out, k?

GABRIELLE

K, I'll try

**From:** Prianka Basak
**To:** Cecily Anderson, Gabrielle Katz
**Subject:** WAHHHHHH

Hi, guys—

My mom took my phone away because she saw what happened on the text with Victoria. That app really works! Also, Victoria's mom emailed my mom. And Mr. Carransey called me in. UGH. I am in so much trouble. I don't even know when I can get my phone back. I feel so lost without it. WAH. So sad over here.

xoxo Pri

# Cecily, Gabrielle

CECILY

Pri doesn't even get that I'm mad @ her . . .

Doesn't she c how dumb it was 2 do that & how much she hurt V's feelings

Gabs, hello

R u there

GABRIELLE

I'm here . . .

IDK what 2 say.

It's all messed up

I'm scared of writing anything bc of my mom w/ that app!

CECILY

Ugh ok

Bye xox

**From:** Gabrielle Katz
**To:** Colin Hayes
**Subject:** no subject

colin,

hey. i'm emailing you instead of texting bc my mom has that app to see my phone and i'm freaked out. meet me at my locker tomorrow before school and i will tell you who sent the note.

—gabby

**From:** Prianka Basak
**To:** Gabrielle Katz
**Subject:** Mad at me, too?

Gabs,

Are you mad at me, too? It was an accident. I didn't mean to hurt Victoria's feelings. Can we talk?

I miss you!

Pri

## Cecily, Mara

C   M

CECILY

My friends turned crazy, I think . . .

MARA

?!?

CECILY

Pri got in major trouble bc she was mean to Victoria on text

She got her phone taken away & promise u won't tell any1—Gabs is the 1 who sent note to Colin.

MARA

⁉️⁉️ OMG OMG OMG OMG

CECILY

PROMISE YOU WILL NOT TELL ANY1.

MARA

👄👄👄 = sealed.

CECILY

Com

E over after school tomw?

MARA

# MEMO

**From:** Mr. Carransey, Principal Yorkville Middle School
**To:** ALL SIXTH-GRADE STUDENTS, ALL SIXTH-GRADE PARENTS
**Re:** Valentine's Day Dance

Dear sixth graders and parents:

The Valentine's Day dance has been canceled. Students were warned about the consequences of their behavior, but the social cruelty continued. It's more than that—I see you when you are talking to one another, and sometimes you do not even lift your heads to talk face-to-face. Your eyes are glued to your phones. Do you value your phones more than social decency? Spend some time thinking about this.

Sincerely,
Edward Carransey
Principal
Yorkville Middle School

*Be the change you want to see in the world.—Gandhi*

# Colin, Gabrielle

COLIN

R u sure bout that note?

GABRIELLE

Uh huh 👊

COLIN

Doesn't make sense

We r just badminton partners

GABRIELLE

Trust me

COLIN

I don't like her tho . . .

GABRIELLE

So just forget about the note, k

**COLIN**

U r kinda weird . . .

**GABRIELLE**

Am not

GTG

Dear Diary,
I did another dumb thing. I can't even put it in
writing. I think my mom is snooping. Everything
feels terrible. I want to run away.

Love,
Gabby

# Cecily, Mara

**MARA**

So much fun hangin w/ u yest 👏👏👏

**CECILY**

I KNOW

Good thing we r normal 1s in our groups so we can hang 👧👧 👧👧

**MARA**

Totally

Every1 is bonkers

But I have to tell u something . . .

Promise not to freak? 👹 🙏

CECILY

Ummmm

MARA

Sooo Gabby's locker is next to mine & I heard her talking to Colin before 1st period . . .

CECILY

Yeah

MARA

She told him u sent him an anonymous love letter or something?

• • •

CECILY

What

Me?

R u sure you heard right

**MARA**

Yeah . . . It was like she didn't know what to say or something . . . Seemed SO SO SO weird 😵 😵 😵

**CECILY**

Ummm I am so confused

People r just getting weirder  😧😧😧😧😧

**MARA**

I KNOW 👽👽👽👽👽

**CECILY**

Let's run away 2gether 2 our own island or something  🙇🙏🙇🙏

**MARA**

OK!!!! 👍👍👍👊

**CECILY**

I am so embarrassed tho

I don't like Colin!!

172

We still have to play badminton together

What should I do??

MARA

Pretend u don't know . . . Just act normal
🧜‍♀️🧜‍♀️🧜‍♀️

CECILY

UGH this is soo annoying

Does any1 care about getting the dance
back 😫😨👭👭🧜‍♀️🎆🎏

MARA

IDK

CECILY

I want to skip school 4ever

I am in a fight with Prianka

& now Colin thinks I like him

& tbh this is soooooo awkward

MARA

It'll be ok

Just hang w/ me

CECILY

M girls + C? 🐺🐺

MARA

Hee hee

We don't even call ourselves that anymore

K, nighty night 😘 😘 😘

SWAK 😘 😘

**From:** Prianka Basak
**To:** Cecily Anderson
**Subject:** I MISS YOUUUUU

Hi, Cece,

I miss you so much. I don't know when I'm getting my phone back. Please talk to me, Cece. I wrote Victoria an apology letter. I need to tell you what happened at Bal Vihar on Sunday. I think Vishal wants to go out with me. What should I do? I really miss you. . . .

xoxo Pri

Prianka Basak's Sad Missing Her Phone Poetry
Book

Poem 1
Prianka is sad
Her phone is gone
When will she get it back?
How does anyone survive without a phone?
I wish I knew

**From:** Gabrielle Katz
**To:** Prianka Basak
**Subject:** CAN YOU USE THE PHONE AT
ALL??

Pri,

I'm writing this from computer lab. I really

need to talk to you in private. Can you use the phone? Like a landline? It is really important.

xo Gabs

## READING LOG

V— Here are my reading log pages. So sorry again about that group text. I feel so bad for Auggie. Middle school is hard enough with a regular face, ya know? —G

I know—but even saying "regular face" sounds insensitive, to be honest. Thanks for apologizing. Here are my pages. —V

**From:** Prianka Basak
**To:** Gabrielle Katz
**Subject:** NO PHONES ALLOWED

gabs,

i'm not allowed to call/text/anything. i am only allowed on email to get school assignments, so even this is illegal. meet me in front of the cafeteria before 1st period tomorrow and we can talk. me and vishal are a real couple! omg. too bad I can't talk to him at all outside of school or bal vihar. BOO HOO.

smooches, pri

## Cecily, Gabrielle

CECILY

I am so so so mad at u btw

I figured u'd at least tell me urself what u did, but I had to hear from like 3 other peeps

GABRIELLE

I am so sorry, Cece

I wanted to tell him it was me

But at last second I froze & I was like "well, Cece can handle anything" so I said u

But I am so so sorry

CECILY

DON'T CRYING CAT FACE ME!!!!!

WE ARE PAST EMOJIS RIGHT NOW

I don't like Colin

I don't like any boy right now

I need a break, ok

Please don't text me anymore

GABRIELLE

Please please please forgive me

I will do anything

CECILY

I SAID DON'T TEXT ME ANYMORE

---

## Poem 2
We wish and wish and wish and wish
But some things don't come true
It is the way of life
Might as well get used to it

---

**From:** Gabrielle Katz
**To:** Colin Hayes
**Subject:** Hi

Dear Colin,

I need to tell you something. It was me who wrote the note. I don't know why I lied and said it was Cecily. I guess because you are badminton partners and it seemed believable and I got scared. I have liked you for a really long time. I guess that's all I have to say.

From, Gabby

Hi, Cece, I'm writing you this note because you said not to text you anymore, but you didn't say I couldn't pass you a note between classes. I am so so sorry about what I did. I don't have a good excuse, really, but I got scared. Can we please talk? xoxo Gabs

Dear Gabs, I know you're sorry. Thanks for apologizing. But honestly, I just can't deal with the drama right now. I'm still really mad and I think I just need a break from you and Pri for a bit. —Cece

## Gabrielle, Victoria

**VICTORIA**

Gabby, r u there 🐱 🐺 🐱 🐱

**GABRIELLE**

Yeah

Hi

**VICTORIA**

Just wanted to say that I saw u crying after school 2day by the bus line

I felt really bad but I didn't know what 2 say

So I'm texting u now 2 check in 🖤 💔 💞 🖤 💔 💞

**GABRIELLE**

Oh, thanx

That's really sweet of u

U r def the Summer of Yorkville

VICTORIA

R u ok

& YAY!

Summer is my fave char in WONDER!!!!!! "If you can get through middle school without hurting anyone's feelings, that's really cool beans."

GABRIELLE

Seriously

I guess my friends & I can't do that . . .
Cecily is mad at me & Pri still doesn't have
her phone but all she cares about is Vishal
& I sent Colin that anonymous note & then
I admitted it was me, & I haven't heard
anything from him since & my mom said we
are definitely moving this summer . . .

VICTORIA

Wow that was a long text

Longest text I've ever gotten

That is prob so dorky to say

😎 😎 😎 😎

GABRIELLE

LOL not dorky

VICTORIA

Maybe Colin doesn't know what 2 say

Boys r kinda slow LOL 😂 😂

GABRIELLE

LOL. Maybe

VICTORIA

It'll all work out 🤞🖐️🤞🤛

GABRIELLE

U think? 😳

VICTORIA

Yes

Def

If u ever want 2 talk or uh text I'm here

GABRIELLE

LOL

Thanx, Victoria

## Cecily, Mara

So do u think I should write that email 2 the grade about putting our phones in Mr. Carransey's office 4 a day

MARA

I think it's a great idea

CECILY

His secretary said she'd put out a box and just make sure all phones are labeled

I think it'll make a strong point

MARA

Def

CECILY

I'm nervous—what if no1 does it?

187

Well, send the email & then ask people to respond if they're gonna do it

Ya know

Good idea 👍

**From:** Cecily Anderson
**To:** 6th Grade Students
**Subject:** Phones and texting

Dear classmates:

By now you have all heard that Mr. Carransey canceled the Valentine's Day dance because of social cruelty in the school. It is in the other grades, too, but mostly our grade. I thought we could all prove that we value each other more than our phones, by doing a phone drop. We'll all put our phones in a box in Mr. Carransey's office and leave them there overnight. Hopefully he will be pleased by this and realize that we are done with social cruelty and texting and social media, and he will reconsider having the dance. Please reply and let me know if you will be participating. Then I will provide instructions.

Sincerely,
Cecily Anderson, 6th grade rep

## Cecily, Mara

CECILY

OMG—have gotten so many responses 👏👏

MARA

Everyone is gonna do it? 🙏

CECILY

I think so!

I'll give it a few more days

MARA

Yay we are totes getting our dance back

CECILY

YAAAAA

---

Dear Diary,

Colin still hasn't responded about the note. Cecily isn't talking to me. I am embarrassed to bring it up to Pri. So embarrassed.

Love,
Gabby

**PRIANKA**

Guess who has her fone back???? 👏 📱 👏

**GABRIELLE**

Welcome back 👧🏻💃🏻👧🏻💃🏻

**CECILY**

Welcome back but I'm still not talking 2 either of u

**GABRIELLE**

Right, well, this is texting not talking 😂😂😂

**CECILY**

BLARGH 😡😡😡😡

**GABRIELLE**

Cece, I liked ur idea of the phone drop

PRIANKA

I liked it 2

CECILY

Thanks

GABRIELLE

How'd you get ur phone back, Pri?

*Cecily HAS LEFT THE CHAT*

## Prianka, Gabrielle

P    G

GABRIELLE

Sheesh she's really not talking to us

PRIANKA

Guess not

GABRIELLE

Soooooo how'd u get it back???

**PRIANKA**

Well

Long story

Ready? ✏️ ✏️ ✏️ ✏️

**GABRIELLE**

Yesssss

**PRIANKA**

Well, my parents said I couldn't get it back until I realized what I'd done & how my words affect others so I was like, uhhhh . . .

But then I realized what I could do

In my meeting with Mr. Carransey I told him I could start a task force

Like a group

**GABRIELLE**

I don't get it

**PRIANKA**

Like we could have meetings and stuff 2 make sure every1 is being nice & using their phones for good

**GABRIELLE**

Ummmm ok sure 👍👍👏👏

**PRIANKA**

Isn't it genius

We r going 2 start in march!! 👏👏👏

**GABRIELLE**

I guess?

**PRIANKA**

GABS, it is genius 😎😎😎

**GABRIELLE**

Congrats, Pri

U got ur phone back & u r helping humanity 2 . . . 🌍🌍🌍

PRIANKA

YES YES YES!!!!! ☮ ☮ ☮ ☮ ☮ ☮

Reason #6 to stay in
Yorkville:
Sometimes we do the
wrong thing, but we
always fix it.
♡ xoxo

DEAR PRIANKA:
I GOT THESE LETTERS AT THE
COMIC BOOK STORE. AREN'T THEY
COOL? IT HELPS TO PASS THE
TIME IN STUDY HALL. DO U THINK
WE'LL GET THE DANCE BACK?
-VISHAL

Cece, Hope you go to your locker before lunch to see this note!!! I just walked by Mr. Carransey's office, and the box for phones is almost full! GO YOU! xoxo Mara

**From:** Colin Hayes
**To:** Gabrielle Katz
**Subject:** Note

Dear Gabby,

Thanks for telling me about the note. Sorry I forgot to write back for so long. It's cool that you like me.

—Colin

## Prianka, Gabrielle

GABRIELLE

What does that email mean??

PRIANKA

IDK

Guess he thinks it's cool

GABRIELLE

Do. u understand 👦👦🏃🏃?

PRIANKA

Not really

Hee hee

GABRIELLE

UGH

BYE

Cece, I am so so so sorry about the whole thing with the note. Please forgive me. Meet me outside the cafeteria for lunch. I am so so sorry.
I love you. Gabs

## MEMO

**From:** Mr. Carransey, Principal, Yorkville Middle School
**To:** ALL SIXTH-GRADE STUDENTS

Please meet in the auditorium after third period.

Thank you,
Edward Carransey
Principal
Yorkville Middle School

*Be the change you want to see in the world.—Gandhi*

## Cecily, Mara

**MARA**

OMG, CECILY!

U did it

U got the dance back

**CECILY**

Well, we ALL did it

Every1 dropped their phones

The whole grade

**MARA**

I can't believe it

SO EXCITED THO

Me too!!!!

Dear Cece,
Congrats on all your hard work on getting the dance back. I just want to say sorry again for the note thing. It was inexcusable. Please find with this note a bag of peanut m&ms. Your favorite. Please forgive me.
xoxo Gabs

# BFFAE 4 REAL

**CECILY**

OK, u guys, thx 4 all the notes & emails & everything

I'm done being in a fight

🐰🐰 🐰🐰 🐰🐰 🐰🐰

**PRIANKA**

4 real? 💕 💕 💕 💕

**GABRIELLE**

YEAH?? ❤️ ❤️ ❤️ ❤️ ❤️ ❤️ ❤️ ❤️ ❤️ ❤️ ❤️ ❤️ ❤️ ❤️ ❤️

**CECILY**

I missed u guys

But here r new ground rules

**READY?**

PRIANKA

YUP ✓ ✓

GABRIELLE

YUPPPPPP ✓ ✓

CECILY

1. No texting fights
2. Make sure u know who u r group texting
3. No lying about secret admirer notes
4. No M girl bashing
5. Gabby is not allowed 2 move
6. We must have fun at the dance 2gether

GABRIELLE

WORKS 4 ME! ✓ ✓

PRIANKA

ME 2!!!!! ✓ ✓

# Vishal, Prianka

VISHAL

So dance is back on . . .

PRIANKA

VISHAL

R u allowed 2 go?

PRIANKA

VISHAL

Cool

PRIANKA

R u going?

VISHAL

Yea

V— Thanks for being so caring. —Gabby

♡ ♡ ♡

No problem. Glad you made up with your friends. Can we hang at the dance? —V

♡ ♡ ♡ ♡

Definitely. Sorry I'm passing notes in class, but I didn't want you to think I was ignoring you.

Thanks! xoxo

♡ ✳ ♡ ✳

# DANCE GIRLZZZZZZZ

P  C  G  V

**VICTORIA**

What is every1 wearing 2 the dance

**PRIANKA**

Black flare-y dress and silver flats

**CECILY**

Kelly green dress w/ tie waist.

Silver flats w/ tiny heel! 👏🏻

**GABRIELLE**

Pink & white polka-dot dress (trust me, vv cute!) & silver mini-heels

Guess we love silver!!

U?

**VICTORIA**

That all sounds amazing!!!

I think I'm going 2 wear this pale blue dress and—wait for it—silver platforms!!!

**CECILY**

K, it's official

We are now the Silver Girls! 🙌 🙌

**GABRIELLE**

YEAHHHHH 👊 👊 👊 👊

**PRIANKA**

Nice, Cece! 💪 💪 💪

**VICTORIA**

I LUV IT!!!!!!!! 😎 😎 😎 😎

**From:** Prianka Basak
**To:** Cecily Anderson, Gabrielle Katz
**Subject:** Re: Following my rules

ALL GOOD!

> **From:** Gabrielle Katz
> **To:** Cecily Anderson, Prianka Basak
> **Subject:** Re: Following my rules
>
> Agree! She's my reading log buddy. . . .
>
> > **From:** Cecily Anderson
> > **To:** Gabrielle Katz, Prianka Basak
> > **Subject:** Following my rules
> >
> > See, I am not starting a separate text to you guys without Victoria . . . I am emailing instead. So don't roll your eyes about the Silver Girls thing. I was just trying to be nice and make her feel included. And honestly, she's not that bad. xoxo

Dear Diary,
So I made up with my friends, finally. And Colin was nice about the note. Now all I need to figure out is how to dance with Colin at the Valentine's Day dance. Any ideas?

Love,
Gabby

Reason #7, #8, #9 to stay in Yorkville:
Fireworks at Millbrook Pier on 4th of July, Memorial Day parade down Sullivan Street, the outstanding school system. ♡ xoxo

Dear Diary,

Well, I had my first-ever school dance. And guess what? It was actually fun! I danced with my friends the whole time. Well, we ate pizza, too, and drank soda. But we danced a ton! Colin talked to me, too, but we didn't dance together. No girls danced with boys. But that's okay. And guess what else? My mom said she's putting the moving plan on hold. I guess now all I need to worry about is if Colin likes me back. And what to do for my birthday and also the math midterm. I guess that is a lot to worry about. And now I'm tired. Bye for now.

Love,
Gabby

# SQUAD BFFAE BEST GIRLS EVA

PRIANKA

I'm not being exclusive but I wanted 2 send a simple text 2 the 2 of u & say gnight & luv you guys & can we please be BFF forever?

GABRIELLE

OF COURSE

I LUV U GUYS

CECILY

YESSSSSS

PRIANKA

 CPG 4EVA!!

# GLOSSARY

**2** to

**2gether** together

**4** for

**4eva** forever

**any1** anyone

**BFF** best friends forever

**BFFAE** best friends forever and ever

**b-room** bathroom

**b/t** between

**c** See

**caf** cafeteria

**comm** committee

**comp** computer

**DEK** don't even know

**def** definitely

**diff** different

**disc** discussion

**fab** fabulous

**fac** faculty

**fave** favorite

**fone** phone

**fyi** for your information

**gtg** gotta go

**gn** good night

**gnight** good night

**hw** homework

**ICB** I can't believe

**IDC** I don't care

**IDK** I don't know

**IHNC** I have no clue

**IK** I know

**ILY** I love you

**ILYSM** I love you so much

**JK** just kidding

**K** okay

**L8r** later

**LMK** let me know

**lol** laugh out loud

**luv** love

**n e way** anyway

**nums** numbers

**obv** obviously

**obvi** obviously

**OMG** oh my God

**peeps** people

**pgs** pages

**plzzzz** please

**pos** possibly

**q** question

**r** are

**rlly** really

**sci** science

**sec** second

**sem** semester

**scheds** schedules

**SWAK** sealed with a kiss

**TBH** to be honest

**thx** thanks

**tm** tomorrow

**tmrw** tomorrow

**tomrw** tomorrow

**tomw** tomorrow

**totes** totally

**u** you

**ur** your

**vv** very, very

**w/** with

**wb** write back

**w/o** without

**WIGO** what is going on

**whatev** whatever

**wut** what

**wuzzzz** what's

**Y** why

## ACKNOWLEDGMENTS

A million thank-yous going out to: Dave, Aleah, Hazel, all the Greenwalds, all the Rosenbergs, the BWL Library & Tech team, my fabulous editor, Maria, Rebecca, Katherine, Aurora, Amy, Erica, Bethany, Ann, Stephanie, and all the wonderful people at Katherine Tegen Books, superstar agent Alyssa, every single person who has ever read one of my books, and last but not least, all of my fabulous texting buddies. I love you all! XOXOXOXO

**LISA GREENWALD** lives in NYC 🍎 w/ her husband & 2 young daughters 👧👧 👧👧. She ❤️s: 😎 📚 🎨 & 🎧.